# MONSOON
## RENDEZVOUS

I0731917

*A GENESIS PROJECT NOVELLA*

# MARK P.J.NADON

# Thrillers by Mark P.J. Nadon

<u>**Military Thrillers:**</u>

**The Genesis Project**

The Genesis Project (Book 1) – June 2024

Monsoon Rendezvous Novella (Book 1.5) – Winter 2025

Cognitive Breach Novella (Book 1.75) – Forthcoming Winter 2025

**Short Stories**

Operation Sanitation Short Story – August 2024

Operation Tangle Short Story – September 2024

# Post Apocalyptic Thrillers:

## Armageddon's Descendants Trilogy

The Collective (Book 1) – Forthcoming Winter 2025

The Chosen (Book 2) – Forthcoming Summer 2025

The Reckoning (Book 3) – Forthcoming Fall 2025

If you enjoy Mark's books, please consider leaving a review! It means
the world to him and helps others find his books

Monsoon Rendezvous: A Genesis Project Novella (Book 1.5)

Copyright © [2025] by [Mark PJ Nadon]

All rights reserved.

Visit the author's website at www.markpjnadon.ca

The story, all names, characters, and incidents portrayed in this book are fictitious. No identification with actual persons (living or deceased), places, buildings, and products is intended or should be inferred.

Cover designed by MiBlart

First Published: January 2025

ISBN (Electronic Book): 978-1-7383077-2-2
ISBN (Paperback): 978-1-7383077-7-7

For my son Matthew—may you always
understand the strength it takes to
fight, the courage it takes to love,
and the power of holding on to both.

# Chapter 1

Clara scooped river water into her hand and sipped. For virtual water, it tasted crisp and clean, cold as it ran down her chin and soaked her shirt.

"What do you think?" Doctor Kendra smiled, staring up at the waterfall splashing down a hundred yards away. "I never get used to it. It's so beautiful. Perfect. Peaceful. How does it make you feel?"

"Sad," Clara said.

"Sad?"

"It's not real. In an hour, the dream will end, and I'll be back at Genesis," Clara said, dipping her hand into the water and pulling up sand from the bottom of the river to run through her fingers. "My throat will be dry, my tears will be real, and all I'll have is this memory. It's kind of like a drug. I'm having a taste, and soon I'll want another fix."

"You know you can't re—"

"I know. One time only. A favor from Colonel Marks after what he did to our family. One hour to solve all my feelings," she chuckled. The only thing she'd solved in this hour session was the question of how much she had loved Blake. She must have loved him deeply for her to exchange the career she'd built for herself overseas for a desk job and a monotonous life as a housewife. She loved Sophia without question.

She was her world. But she'd given up everything for Blake, and there was nothing left for her.

"One hour *here*," Doctor Kendra corrected. "I'll be reachable for follow-up."

*In three months.* "Right."

"How is Blake?"

"You should know. You see the real Blake more than I do," Clara snapped, instantly regretting her tone. It wasn't Doctor Kendra's fault. It was hers. And Blake's. Mostly Blake's. He was always on a mission in his head. He never came home, and she no longer believed he ever would. The army had sucked him in and he'd married every man he came in contact with, putting them above her and Sophia. She'd thought leaving the Unit at Delta and having a nine-to-five job would spark their love again. It hadn't. The Genesis Project gave him more PTSD than he'd ever gotten on operations, living nightmares with soldiers to cure their own trauma. *I thought we might find each other again, until—*

"The sequence is ready. Are you?" Dr. Kendra asked. Her concentration seemed only half on Clara and half on her soaking feet, squishing sand between her toes.

Clara's lips parted to say yes, but then she hesitated. *Am I ready?*

"It's your dream, your memory," Doctor Kendra said, carefully stepping through the water to stand next to Clara. "The AI cataloged your dreams for three nights. Nothing can go wrong. You're just reliving the dream. It's not a nightmare. You've been there before. Remember when you said it was one of the best times of your life?"

*Best time of my life. The most exhilarating. Before his marriage to the teams.* Clara hated admitting to herself that she missed those moments with Blake more than she missed moments with Sophia. Maybe it was because she and Sophia were so close, and every moment felt wonderful and special. Moments with Blake had become dreadful and disconnected. Her parents thought tough times would strengthen their marriage. They hadn't.

"I'm afraid to get angrier. Or sadder. I know everyone means well by giving me this opportunity; nobody gets to do this. But what if I relive those memories and come back even more bitter and frustrated? Instead of finding the spark that you seem to think I'll find." Clara sat in the frigid water, her muscles tensing as the cold took her breath away. *So incredibly real. No wonder Blake had a hard time reliving nightmares every day.*

But she didn't need to make excuses for him. He made enough of his own. Though, experiencing it, no matter how real he described it, was...different. There's no question how horrible the things he must have seen were. Then seen them again, and again.

"It's okay to be angry," Doctor Kendra sat next to her and gasped when her butt hit the water. "Oh my God, that's so cold. You'd think we could have programmed warm bath water instead of this." Doctor Kendra laughed, goosebumps popping up on her arms and legs. She had no body fat to act as a layer between her skin and the cold. Only brown blood cells, but maybe they didn't work in this environment. Would the Genesis know if she had a tolerance for freezing? Or would all the ones and zeros just make assumptions?

"Blake went through the same memory sequence, and it opened his eyes to a lot of things. I can't say for sure what he'll act on, but I know reliving these emotions gave him a lot to think about." Doctor Kendra lowered herself into the water and lay back, floating. "The right thing for you might be to leave him. Or you might find a reason to work together to heal your marriage after the damage done the last few years."

*Damage I don't know if we can come back from.* "Okay, let's do it," Clara said, hoping the Genesis hadn't tampered with her memory of that insane day.

Dr. Kendra smiled. "I'll be with you the whole time. You'll feel like you're living it again, but I can pull you out if you want, okay?"

Clara nodded. The world went dark as Genesis loaded her dream sequence.

# Chapter 2

Clara pulled Farzana close to her. They pressed up against the stone wall outside the far corner of the hospital. Samira stood a dozen feet away and lowered her gaze to the dirt, probably too shy to ask for a hug. Clara opened her spare arm and waved Samira closer. She dashed into Clara's arms.

*These girls should be at their shelter in place site. I never should have accepted their help.*

"We're going to be fine," Clara said to the girls in Bengali.

"I'm scared of storms," Samira whimpered, her own Bengali much more fluent than Clara's. "Two of my friends died in a storm last year. Arafat and Nusrat. Mom said they died quickly in their sleep. Kabir, he lives down the street, said the house collapsed on them and he *still* hears them screaming. He says their souls are trapped in there forever."

"I'm scared," Farzana echoed with equally crisp Bengali. "I don't want my soul to get trapped, Mrs. Clara. Not forever. I couldn't imagine being in one place that long."

Clara swallowed hard. "I'm sorry you lost your friends, Samira," Clara said. "That's why my team and I are here. To help prevent anyone from dying."

"My uncle Moinuddin died, I think four years ago. I didn't know him very well. Dad was the most upset. He had sad eyes for a really long time. Still kinda does." Farzana's face drooped as if she was mimicking her father's face. "I asked mom why he was so sad, and she said because he—"

"Mom lost half her fingers last year," Samira said, not one to be outdone. "She can't carry water home from the stream anymore. My brother Jahid," Samira looked up at Clara, "he's had to carry twice as much water. He grumbles every day. It's hard on his shoulders, he says. I think he just wants to play cricket. The Tigers have a junior training camp he wants to be invited to. He's in denial about how bad he is."

"He's not bad," Farzana said with a little pizzazz.

"Okay. Okay," Clara laughed. "The storm isn't so bad and we're helping get people ready for it, right?" Although the wind had picked up far more than it should have so early in their predictions. Clara reminded herself to check the radar on her phone after seeing the girls off.

Samira rubbed the logo on Clara's bright red jacket, depicting what used to be the silhouette of a person with arms out overhead, now turned shades of mud from playing with the kids.

"You give big...ugs, jus...him." Heavy winds blew in from the north, cutting out Samira's words. Sand came with it, and they all covered their faces with their hands to block the stab of a thousand needles.

"It...won't...las...long," Clara shouted, her words mostly lost in the storm's power. It must have been the heaviest gust yet, and suddenly Clara didn't feel as confident about their safety as she'd sounded a moment ago. The storm didn't care if she was from a first world country and had a good job, stable home with her parents, and money in investments. It only destroyed.

The wind died, and the girls shook for a long time, like leaves rattling in the trees. Clara knew these patterns too well. The sudden violent gusts were characteristic of microbursts—massive downdrafts of cold air that could flip cars and tear buildings apart in minutes. They often came before the monsoons, nature's warning shot that went unheeded too often. Last year, a microburst had torn through a village forty miles south, leveling everything in its path. Clara pushed the memory away, not wanting to think about what these winds might mean. Clara didn't dare move. She wrapped the girls tighter in her arms, taking as much solace from them as they were from her. The storm didn't care about predictions or preparations. It would come when it wanted, as fierce as it pleased.

"All okay?" Elijah poked his head around the wall, pressing down on his wide-brimmed straw hat like it might blow away any second. The hat had lost so much straw over the years, it should have disintegrated in the wind. He forced a toothy smile, but his teeth were more brown than white. Samira drew in tighter to Clara when Eijah's gangly arms reached for her.

"We're fine," Clara said to Elijah in English, leaning forward to shield the girls from his touch. Although Elijah meant well and traveled with her team in Southern Asia, there was something about the way his eyes lingered on them a fraction of a second too long, and the way he licked his lips when he shifted his gaze, even if he had lips as dry and chapped as the earth of a paddy field awaiting the monsoon. His mannerisms were habit and she didn't think he meant to creep anyone out, but he did.

"Good. Very Good. Would you like me to take de girls back to de shelter?" he said with a heavy Nepali accent. He insisted on speaking English so he could travel more with the team. He'd improved over the years he'd been with them but was far from fluent.

Samira tightened her grip on Clara's arm. Clara pretended not to notice.

"No. I'll take them. Thank you."

"Dis a long way," he said. "Dere are a lot of preparations to make dat I can't, no? Important tings for you to do, no? Is no problem. I take girls to de shelter." His toothy smile grew a little. Clara knew he just wanted to help. But the girls in the village didn't trust men. Too many girls walking alone had been pulled into the forest and raped. Some girls were never seen again. Mothers made their daughters promise never to get near a man they didn't know.

"Thank you. I'll take them," she said. Their village, Shaplapalli, was nestled a good nine miles away, much of it dirt roads or trails even cars had a tough time traversing. Still, it had a school built with brick and was the designated shelter in place for the two girls and their village. They should be there now, but the girls had appeared at the hospital entrance earlier, eyes bright with eagerness to help. When Samira said they could carry boxes just like the big people, Clara hadn't had the heart to turn them away. She should have sent them straight to the shelter in the bus, but their excited smiles and rolled-up sleeves had worn down her better judgment. She hadn't known then how the weather would turn. Now someone would be looking for them, and they were nine miles from where they should be.

"Okay. Okay. I here to help if you need'it."

"Yes. Thank you." Clara stood and dusted off her pants the best she could with the girls still glued to her side. She took a few steps, breaking free. They followed closely behind, never raising their eyes to meet Elijah's.

Clara took the girls to the Save the Children (STC) command tent. The vehicles belonged to the organization, and she'd need approval to drive the girls home. Given the monsoon was expected overnight and nobody would be at the hospital to watch over them, she figured she'd get approval. Hopefully her team would pick up her storm prep slack and have the medical supplies ready for distribution.

"It's going to be loud in there," Clara said to the girls before they entered the tent. She heard the voices inside, all of them shouting over each other in English, one louder than the last. Typical evening at the command tent. She was glad to be a team lead and not a section manager. "Stay close and keep quiet, okay?"

Both girls nodded.

She lifted the tent flap and stepped inside, only to run into a man with his head turned away from her as he stepped into her path. It was like hitting a wall. She bounced back into the girls and they both yelped. The man turned and let out a good-natured laugh.

"Where'd you come from?" Blake asked in English. His overgrown beard and poofy hair made him the most unprofessional person in the tent, although his eyes sparkled with a confidence larger than he was. She'd disliked him from the moment they met a few days ago because he'd commandeered one of their vehicles and taken supplies into India. No way she'd let him do it again. Sure, everyone needed help, but their mission was here, not in India. She resented all the extra hours she'd worked to compensate for the supplies he'd taken that day. Also, he wasn't a member of their team. She didn't really know him, and Raj had redirected her inquiries to people that never answered their messages.

Her resentment was only stoked when she spotted the keys in Blake's hand.

"I need the vehicle to bring these girls to the shelter. You'll have to wait," Clara said, her tone firm and arms crossed as she met his gaze

"Wait?" His eyebrows rose, and the tone in their contortion shifted from amusement to seriousness as he glanced from Clara to the girls and back. "I'm sorry, I can't. It's time sensitive. The hospital is a safe place to stay with the girls for now."

The wind picked up again and the tent buckled. Clara pulled the girls inside and closed the flap, but it wouldn't be long before the gusts blew the tent away, even with the sandbags and pegs holding it down. The hospital was the nearest shelter for many people, but they packed it tighter than the tent, so many people had remained home waiting in their rickety shanties to get killed. STC kept the status quo until there were no alternatives.

Everyone in the room seemed to hold their breath. Even while holding her breath, Clara smelled the pungent body odor of STC men who had sweated too much and hadn't changed their clothes. She gagged, doing her best to pretend she was fine. *No wonder God gave us olfactory fatigue.*

When the wind dissipated, the girls opened the flap as if to look outside and Clara breathed in a little of the fresh air, thankful to them for not making her crawl out on her hands and knees; if smells could kill.

"You should go inside before the girls get hurt," Blake said, crossing his muscled arms, the veins running up to his biceps and thick shoulders. She felt her face burn red, mostly from her anger. The noise in the room returned, forcing everyone to shout to be overheard.

"I need a vehicle to take these girls home. You can't have it." Clara took a step forward, standing as tall as she could to prove she wasn't intimidated by his six-foot figure. At five-nine, she could easily stand toe to toe with him.

He shook his head and twisted around to the other people in the room.

*Fine. Good. Did he understand?* Clara shuffled past a few of the men to get to Raj, her section manager. Raj was surrounded by men and women, all talking at him at the same time. When he saw Clara, he winked at her and tugged lightly at his hair: the sign for help.

Sweat bore down his face like he'd been splashed with a bucket of water. She smiled, wanting nothing to do with his entourage. Some she recognized as team leaders just like her. Others she'd never met; they dressed well above her pay grade.

She took a moment to decide if she should skip the line ahead of the other team leaders. Rohan constantly thought food was most vital for people. Nina liked to talk for the sake of talking, and she loved to flick her hair back every few sentences as if a photographer was taking pictures of her from the other side of the conversation. Emily shifted awkwardly, her mouth opening and closing whenever she might get a word in, only to be cut off by the next voice.

Clara made a hand signal, twisting her wrist three times like she was starting a car to ensure he got the hint. He pointed behind her and she turned to an apologetic-looking Blake.

"Sorry," he shrugged. "The girls will be safe here."

Clara scoffed and pushed past him, leading the girls outside the tent. The road to the hospital was closed, so no vehicles could pass without police permission, but walking wouldn't be a problem—aside from the exposure. The wind picked up again, stronger than before, nearly knocking Clara off her feet. The girls tugged at her arms, crying now. *Goddamn Blake. If you'd just let us use the damn vehicle, it wouldn't take more than an hour to get the girls home.* Rain lashed against her skin like tiny bullets. Clara dragged the girls into the emergency room, stumbling through the main doors and immediately colliding with a chaotic crowd. The place was absolutely overrun. The police wouldn't know what to do. If an actual emergency came...Clara hoped she wouldn't be there to see it.

The building rattled dust and debris from the ceiling. A few light fixtures plummeted to the ground, smashing atop people standing below. Everyone screamed, looking for a place to retreat, but there was nowhere to go. Clara glanced outside and saw a mailbox fly past the door. She gained the humbling knowledge that even if they'd won the keys from Blake, they weren't going anywhere. *What the hell are you still doing out there, Raj?* He needed to get everyone inside.

The girls continued to cry, along with many of the people in the hallway and waiting areas.

Clara kneeled and pulled the girls closer to her. "I'm going to check on everyone in the tent. Make sure they're safe. You'll be safe here, okay? Stay together and stay here. I'll be back in a few minutes."

Before she lost her nerve, Clara tore away from them and headed for the exit. The automatic doors opened, and the wind blew Clara backwards. People shouted at her not to go out. A few cursed at her, probably for putting them all in danger, but she couldn't translate their fast Bengali with so much noise. She ducked low, her arm up to cover her face, and marched toward the tent.

Except, when she looked in the place the tent was just standing, nothing and no one but sandbags lay on the ground in a rough rectangle.

"What are you doing? Get inside," a gruff voice shouted at her. Blake took her forearm and pulled her back toward the hospital.

Clara jerked her arm backward but was helpless to break his vice grip. "They're out there," she screamed. "Everyone in the tent. The tent's gone. But they're out there."

The wind died as quickly as it had come, like a blow drier turning on and off. The deafening noise turned silent so fast she questioned for a moment if she'd lost her hearing. Blake halted and released her hand. He glanced up at the dark skies, sniffing like he could smell the next blast in the air.

"What happened to them?" Clara said, her hands shaking. "They were all here a few minutes ago. All of them. Microbursts weren't supposed to hit until tomorrow, early in the morning. How did this happen?" She covered her mouth as if to stifle a scream. They couldn't be far. They'd probably left the tent before it blew away.

"Clara," Blake said, taking a firm grip on her shoulders and forcing her to look into his eyes. "You don't want to see. Go back to the hospital."

# Chapter 3

Telling her not to look only drew her eyes to the side of the hospital where she'd taken cover with Farzana and Samira. The tent lay pressed against the building, and a pair of legs with olive cargo pants stuck out from beneath the tent. The feet were pointed in opposite directions and not moving. Near the legs was a puddle of dark liquid. Clara screamed, twisted away from Blake, and ran to the tent. She tried to lift the flap or raise the bar off the legs, but it was too heavy with the material collapsed on itself.

"Raj? Raj are you okay? Help me," she shouted at Blake.

Blake pulled up on the tent's support beam far enough for Clara to peak underneath. Her lip quivered when she saw several more people trapped, bunched up like trash in a can. *The wind doesn't care who you are.*

"Clara?" Raj said, his voice weak and groggy.

"Raj." Relief poured into her lungs as she took a deep breath and let happy tears run down her cheeks.

Several voices turned the quiet aftermath of the storm into a frenzy of panic and shouting, some from inside the tent, probably just realizing what had happened, and several from behind her. She crawled to Raj as people arrived to help lift the tent higher, slipped off her jacket and draped it over him to keep him warm.

"What happened?" Raj said, blinking slowly. His legs were definitely broken—crushed at the femurs. He'd be screaming if he could feel the pain, but that would come later once the shock wore off. She'd seen it many times before. Most of her first aid training focused on broken bones because it was the most common injury outside minor cuts and bruises, which only needed a quick bandage and often got left for later. Treat the worst injuries for people that were most likely to survive, is how STC taught to triage. She hated triage, which is why she never accepted a promotion to section manager. They made hard decisions, prioritizing life and death with quick visuals and team reports. Her training and judgement told her to prioritize the people at the back of the tent that didn't have crushed legs, but this was Raj; it was personal.

"Unexpected wind," Clara said to Raj, forcing a smile. The same smile she'd perfected through her years with STC—not so big that people think you're too happy to be there during a terrible situation, but big enough for them to think everything is going to be okay. "Nobody saw it coming."

"Eh, all okay, boss?" Elijah said, kneeling on the ground with a tent pole over his shoulder, keeping it from crashing down on her. "Leg petty bad. Bes' get doctor."

Raj blinked slowly, closing his eyes completely for a moment before opening them again. He gritted his teeth. The shock was over and the pain was doing its thing.

"Do know dis man?" A nurse pulled in beside Clara with a stretcher and bag, forcing Elijah to step aside. She checked Raj's pulse then shined a light in his eyes. "He needs out here. Now," she said, not waiting for Clara to answer the first question. If the nurses here triaged the same way her team did, that meant Raj might be the worst of the group but still likely to survive.

"His name is Raj," Clara said, but the nurse wasn't listening. She was shouting instructions at her partner in Bengali. The nurses quickly dragged him onto the stretcher and wheeled him in through the front door.

"You did everything you could," Blake said, his tone robotic as he calmly observed the others be pulled out of the tent, many with only minor cuts. He hadn't looked her in the eyes, smiled weakly, or offered any comfort. Whoever he was, he wasn't trained with STC. She'd suspected, not only given his muscular frame and overgrown beard, but his presence, that he was with another organization. When he walked into a room, he commanded attention but seemed indifferent to whether or not you gave it to him. It was easy to notice him, and just as easy to forget him, except in her case because he'd pissed her off. People had suffered without the supplies she should have gotten to them in that vehicle.

"Many to help," Elijah said, looking behind him into the fold of the tent as he helped a woman walk toward the hospital.

Blake's words played in her mind. *He thinks I did everything I could?*

"Except get everyone inside before the wind hit. I should have known. The gusts were getting stronger. I should have insisted they go inside. Raj would have listened to me and the others would have followed, pecking at him like chickens." *Ugh, why did I say it like that?*

"They wouldn't have listened," Blake said and stepped back into the flurry of people beneath the tent, all helping to lift pieces of the tent away to free the remaining people trapped beneath.

*Raj wouldn't have broken legs if I had said something.* Clara followed Blake, standing next to him to help hold a tent post so the paramedics could get in and out without worry. Her arms screamed at her to let go. She stubbornly held on. Blake grunted, his biceps twice the size they had been resting.

Before the paramedics finished, the wind picked up again. Clara hadn't checked the radar and had no idea what was happening. Had a wind shear caused more microbursts? They shouldn't last more than fifteen minutes. She didn't know exactly how long it had been, but it felt like fifteen minutes had passed since she'd stepped outside. *The wind doesn't care about probabilities and averages.*

"In. Inside. Danger wind," the paramedic shouted.

Blake shook his head. "There are more people trapped in there."

"We come back when wind no strong. No needy to others get hurt," the paramedic said. Her voice was sharp, piercing the wind to be understood.

Clara couldn't hold on any longer. She released the post, which forced Blake to release his side. As he lowered the post to the ground, the people still trapped shouted from beneath.

"Day safer dere. We not safer." The paramedic darted toward the hospital entrance, her medical bag pulling her to one side and making her movements awkward. Clara let out a frustrated scream, then pushed past the paramedic, racing for the door. A powerful gust slammed her against the brick wall just as she slipped inside, dropping to her knees on the cold floor.

Blake charged in right behind her, a paramedic's bag slung over his shoulder. The weight hardly slowed him. Shouts erupted again, scolding them for opening the door. Clara barely registered the words; the voices were probably the same frightened people who had yelled earlier, more concerned with their own safety than those still stranded outside.

"They're still out there," Clara muttered, though no one seemed to notice. The overhead lights swung violently, their metallic rattle blending with the wind howling through unseen cracks. The walls groaned under the strain, and for a moment, Clara imagined the whole building crumbling around them. It wasn't an impossible thought.

Just yesterday, she had met with a structural engineer while finalizing shelter-in-place plans. The hospital was deemed the best option, but not without risk. Its age made it vulnerable, the rebar likely to fracture under the unrelenting pressure of the storm. If the winds persisted, parts of the building could collapse. That uncertainty was why they had urged people to stay in reinforced schools or town halls in their own communities.

Clara glanced overhead and saw the beam where she'd left the girls waiting for her. Other people had filled the space. A lightning bolt shape made its way up the pillar. She ran over to check on the girls. They weren't there.

"Watch out," Blake shouted and pulled her away from the beam toward reception with incredible strength. The last time she'd been handled like that, she was a child. The post where she'd been standing abruptly collapsed and the ceiling dropped on the people beneath it.

"No!" Clara reached her hand out, as if to pull out the people crushed below.

The noise kicked up a level as people screamed and shoved each other to get as far away from the collapsing ceiling as they could. Blake held Clara in his arms, blocking those who would shove her to escape.

"The girls," Clara said, partly relieved they weren't there and partly afraid she didn't know where they'd gone. They were her responsibility.

"The two you were with?" Blake scanned the room. They'd never find the girls in the chaos. Yelling for them wouldn't do anything. A missing child alert wouldn't carry any weight until the storm cleared. Nurses, doctors and a dozen onlookers went to work digging out the people buried in the rubble.

"Yes. Two little girls. I told them to wait there for me. They're usually really good listeners. Someone must have told them to move." Clara swallowed down her fear.

"We'll find them. Nobody is going anywhere in this storm."

"I have to find them," she declared, and marched to the nearest nurse station, forcing her way through crowds of people. There were no nurses at the desk. They'd probably stopped taking registrations with so many seriously injured people and no infrastructure to support it. She climbed onto the desk and searched for anyone wearing a light-blue uniform.

The building rumbled and the desk she stood on shook. She lost her balance, saw Blake, and fell toward him. He caught her in his arms and lowered her to the ground.

"Thanks," she said. "Again." *Don't need to make a habit of this.*

"Find what you were looking for?" he said, so calm he was a breath of fresh air in all the panic.

"No. I didn't have enough time." She spotted someone in blue out of the corner of her eye and pulled away from Blake to chase the uniform. She shoved her way through the crowd, not wanting to lose sight of the nurse. "Nurse!" she shouted. "*Narso,*" she tried in Bengali. The nurse turned to regard her, then her eyes flashed back to the collapsed ceiling. Clara grit her teeth. She should help the people in the collapse or head to the tent outside, but the girls...*Is there a right thing to do?*

Blake popped up in front of the nurse. With the noise and distance, Clara couldn't hear their exchange. The nurse pointed down the hallway to Clara's left.

"If the girls went to a nurse for help, they'll be down that hallway in the pediatric wing," Blake said when he reached her.

She followed him through the crowd. His broad shoulders created so much space for her to follow that she didn't have to twist to keep up. The pediatric wing was bright and colorful, with shades of orange, yellow, and red painted on the walls. Blake reached the nurses' station and asked the attending nurse if she spoke English.

"Yes. Some."

"Have you seen two little girls?" Clara shot in, stepping in front of Blake. "About this tall? They both had long brown hair, pretty dirty clothes? Their names are Farzana and Samira." The nurse looked blankly at Clara. She repeated her description, taking slight breaks between words and adding a few in Bengali where she could.

The nurse scanned the clipboard at her desk. A long list of names ran down one column. Clara twisted her head to read the names, desperate to find them herself.

"I no tink so," the nurse said.

"Oh, no." Clara covered her mouth and felt her knees buckle again.

But before she let herself collapse, "Ms. Clara?" a voice called from behind them. Clara twisted and found Farzana and Samira standing together.

"Oh, thank God," Clara said. She covered the distance between them in a blink and pulled them into a hug until they both squealed a little from the squeeze.

"Are you okay, Miss Clara?" Samira said in Bengali, like her chest was in a vice.

"I asked you two not to move." But she was so thankful they hadn't listened.

"Nurse Priya found us and made us come here," Farzana said, tears welling in her eyes. "I told her what you said, and she said we had to listen to her now. I said we could wait just a little longer, and she said it was too dangerous. So I fought to—"

"It's okay," Clara laughed. "She was right. You're both safe now."

"What's happening Mrs. Clara? Are we going to die here?" Samira said.

*Straight to the point.* "No, we're not going to die." *I hope I'm not lying to them.* "The storm is stronger than we expected. What's probably happening right now are bursts of wind created from—"

"I think it's over," Blake interrupted. He stared outside into the evening sky. "You see over there? That swirling patch of dark cloud is heading the other way now." In Bengali, Blake said, "You were both very brave. Super brave."

That piece of the storm might have moved on, but Clara knew another could develop any moment given the high winds.

Both girls smiled. Then Samira's face twisted. "Where's it headed? Is my family okay? I want to go home."

Blake placed a hand on Clara's shoulder. "I can take them home after we help sort out what happened here." Blake patted his pocket, and keys jingled.

It seemed the storm had curbed his stubbornness. Clara smiled up at him and mouthed a thank you. She didn't think the local police would allow them on the roads, but if anyone could talk their way to Shaplapalli, it was Blake. He'd ridden off in vehicles that Raj never should have let him take. She'd thought he was high level at the Cyclone Preparedness Programme, but when she met with a few CPP volunteers, they admitted they didn't know him.

"Stay here, okay girls?" Clara said, nervous to leave them again, but she had to help where she could; she was a team lead. Her staff would be looking up to her, and her bosses would be watching her actions.

Nurse Priya agreed to keep an eye on the kids the best she could. She was the only nurse scheduled for the pediatric wing to allow for more nurses during the morning and day shift tomorrow, when the hospital anticipated real chaos.

The girls nodded and rushed back to the play area. Samira picked up Buzz Lightyear and flew him through the air, to infinity and beyond. Farzana colored in a book with slow and careful strokes. Clara couldn't see what she was coloring from where she stood.

"They'll be fine," Blake said. He headed down the hallway, doing a quick shoulder check to see if she followed. He cracked a smile from the right side of his lips and she felt her face flush. *No, I'm not attracted to him. I'm just feeling a lot right now. I'll feel different tomorrow.*

She returned his smile to be polite and followed him into the noise and chaos of the emergency room lobby.

Two police officers stood at the end of the hallway. One of the officers jumped up on the desk and spoke in Bengali like he had a megaphone. "We're sorry, but you can't go beyond this point. The hospital is doing their best to see to all patients that need assistance. Check with the nurse at the desk if you haven't already. The nurses and doctors need the space to do their jobs. You will see a doctor if you need to. Thank you for your patience." The officer repeated the message in English, though it was much shorter and to-the-point. The bickering and arguments decreased by at least half.

Clara and Blake stepped by the officers to enter the lobby. They headed for the nurse at the desk, approaching from the side because of the lineup of people talking over each other in front of her.

"How can we help?" Blake shouted to be heard over the others. Many people quieted, because his voice commanded it. "Are there more injured that need help?"

The nurse shook her head sadly. In Bengali she said, "I don't know what's going on out there. I was told they'd pulled out the people under the pillar. Most of them are fine. A couple didn't make it. We don't have a line of communication going outside, but some nurses and doctors rushed out there a few minutes ago."

Nurses and doctors? Didn't they know how dangerous it still was? Most of the time microbursts lasted only minutes, but this was different. This felt like the real storm was hitting early.

Clara pulled her phone out to check her weather data. *Temporarily out of service in your area.* She wanted to smash the phone on the ground. She paid a premium price for InstaWeather Pro, along with a monthly subscription fee. *What the hell did I pay for if it doesn't work in this shit?* They'd probably blame the storm, which they'd not predicted to start until tomorrow. What irony.

They found the tent pulled away from the wall and several people with no identifying agency markers helping people limp inside. One large man carried a small boy in his arms. The boy cried. He had several scratches on his arm and legs that were probably painful for a boy that young, but he seemed otherwise fine. Where had the boy come from? Had he been in the tent? If Raj was among the worst injured, they'd gotten away easy with this one.

# Chapter 4

"Miss Clara, all okay?" Elijah walked past her with a heavy-set woman's arm draped over his shoulder, headed for the main entrance. He paused when she didn't reply. "All okay?" he said, his accent heavy. The woman said something in Bengali, too fast for Clara to translate.

Blake stepped in and took the woman's other arm to help Elijah. They turned and headed inside before Clara could draft a response. Was she okay? This is what they trained her for, yet she could feel the twitching in her hands and feet.

After helping the people in the tent, Clara returned to the girls and sat with them. The wind had stopped, at least for now, but she still had to get first aid supplies out to Shaplapalli, Shalbanpur, Noborpur and Jalaladiya. Could her team even function at this point? The truck might only have half the supplies needed, but that was better than nothing. This is what STC was here for. Even if they couldn't get all the kits fully packed, she could get half of them out. Raj needed to approve the use of the vehicles, but he was in surgery. She wouldn't be speaking with him until tomorrow, after the storm hit. Who would pack the remaining tents up? There was so much to do.

"Clara?" Blake startled her and she popped up. She might have punched him if she was standing.

"Yeah?" she said after she recovered.

"I'm heading out with the girls. Just making sure you're okay," he said.

*Why would he care if I was okay?* She nodded. "Thanks. Where are you headed? I'll go with you. The girls will feel better." She assumed he'd say back to Chattogram for a flight to wherever he had to go. He didn't seem like a guy who sat on his hands.

He regarded her with a curiosity that made her feel like he was judging her. She didn't like the feeling. Finally, he said, "I'm heading through Shaplapalli on my way west. You can hitch a ride with me and the girls. But it's a one-way until someone from your group can come and get you. It'll be a few days before you get your truck back," he said.

Clara scoffed. Not only was he going to drive off with the supplies meant for helpless villagers when they needed it most, but he wasn't bringing the vehicle back? *Who the hell is this guy? Who does that?* "How about I give you a drive to Shaplapalli and you find your own way from there? I have supplies to—"

"Sorry, that won't work for me." His brows furrowed briefly before his probably fake smile returned.

If he wasn't so goddamn cute...it frustrated the shit out of her. But he'd saved her life and somehow that had created a soft spot she desperately needed to squash.

"I'm leaving in five," he said. "You know where to be if you're coming." He waved for the girls to follow, and they gave a quick nod like they'd heard him, but she didn't think they had.

"Your face is red, Miss Clara," Farzana said with a grin. She pointed at the coloring book. "Just like her!" She held up an image of Belle from *Beauty and the Beast*, her usually kind expression colored over with a dark red face and her brown hair wildly scribbled in. Clara scowled playfully and lunged at Farzana, knocking her off balance and poking her ribs. Both of them erupted in laughter.

Samira rushed over, grinning as Woody's familiar voice, cheerful and drawling like a small-town sheriff, declared, "Reach for the sky!" The girls burst into more giggles at the exaggerated tone.

The joy faded quickly when Clara reminded them it was time to leave. They begged to take the toys and coloring books, but Clara shook her head, glancing at a Bengali sign on the wall: *If you didn't bring it, don't take it home.* Crude, but effective.

They held hands and walked out to the truck. Blake had loaded a large pack into the back and covered it with a tarp, then closed the tailgate and the rear hatch. The wind had used the truck as its personal shake-and-bake bag and so her supplies were a mess, but nothing looked busted, just out of order.

"What's in there?" Clara asked as she opened the quad cab door and peered through the glass at the tarp in the back.

Blake started the truck. "Everyone buckled in?" He must have heard clicks because he didn't wait for them to respond or look back before he popped the truck in drive as if he didn't already know being in a rush in this weather was just asking for disaster. She knew nothing about him, but if Raj trusted him to take a truck and he'd saved her life, he wouldn't knowingly put her in danger. She hopped in the front seat.

A knock on her window made her jump. Elijah stood outside, his hands covering the tops of his eyes as if blocking out the sun to get a look in the truck.

"All okay, boss? Need me? Off to Shaplapalli?" Elijah said Shapla-palli with a perfect accent, not needing to enunciate each syllable or each *l* like most English people did.

"We're okay. Thank you, Elijah."

"All okay in hospital. Need me? Help wit supplies? Many to give and no much time."

Clara glanced over at Blake who shrugged.

"Can't hurt," Blake said.

"Sure, thank you Elijah," Clara sighed, unbuckling her seatbelt. Elijah made for the back door to sit with the girls, but she popped out the front quickly enough to give him pause. A light drizzle pattered against her skin. "I'll sit in the back. Leave the men to the front." She smiled, hoping appealing to his masculinity would prevent anyone from feeling uncomfortable.

"Okay, boss." Elijah jumped in the front seat, fiddling with the buckle before he finally clipped it. When she'd met Elijah, he'd told her he preferred his scooter or his bicycle and bussed otherwise. Private vehicles with seatbelts were an expensive luxury to maintain and fuel.

They didn't drive far before they ran into police blocking the road ahead with their cars and A-frames. Two officers with flashlights loomed in front of their parked truck. One walked to the window and shined his light on their faces. Clara covered her eyes, trying to stop the burn from the intense illumination. The light worked its way through the truck, into the back, and finally stopped at Blake's lap. Blake rolled down the window, letting in a cool breeze with enough moisture to drink from.

"Hello. Road is closed. You have to turn around," the officer said in Bengali, one hand resting on the butt of his pistol. With a drenched poncho and dark eyes, the officer didn't look happy to be there. Neither did their battered sign that they must have put up a few times over after the wind knocked it down.

"Thank you, officer, but I have urgent supplies to get to Shaplapalli," Blake said Shaplapalli as English as she'd ever heard. He seemed to size up the barrier and the other officer, and Clara could feel him thinking hard but had no idea what about. Maybe the officer felt it too.

"Sorry, sir. We cannot guarantee your safety on the road."

The second officer took a few steps toward Elijah's door, his hand gliding against his pistol but not resting on the butt like the other officer. Clara swallowed hard, ready to apologize and tell Blake to turn around, but people in Shaplapalli needed the supplies. It was her job to deliver them.

"I understand. We won't hold you responsible if you let us pass," Blake smiled. "I'll say we came through before the blockade. Nothing for you to worry about." Blake slipped his hand in his pocket. The police officer pulled his pistol a few inches from the holster, pausing when he saw Blake had paper in his hand. *Money?* "For your trouble," he said.

Her eyes wanted to burn a hole through his stupid forehead. *What the fuck, Blake?* They could all be arrested. Then what? Instead of helping people, someone would have to bail them out of jail. The girls would be sent to a foster home until they figured out who their parents were.

Blake shook the officer's hand with the paper between them. The officer did a double take, smiled, and nodded. He flicked his flashlight from the truck to the sign a few times and spoke to the other officer, who seemed indifferent to the exchange and drove the cruiser out of the way. The first officer leaned in.

"Have a nice day, family. Get supplies to Shaplapalli."

Clara scoffed. As if he'd done it out of the kindness of his heart. One universal truth: money talks in every language.

Blake drove through the barrier and continued down the road.

"Are you crazy? Seriously? Bribing police?" she said. "You could have gotten us arrested. What would you have done then?"

Blake eyed Clara through the rear-view mirror, then looked back at the road. "Let's get your supplies to Shaplapalli, okay? That's your mission."

Elijah stared straight ahead, smiling like he wouldn't say a word unless someone asked him to.

"What's your mission?" she snapped. And who *talks* like that? Was he military? What would the military want in a place like this and why would STC care?

He smiled his smug, irritating smile. "Classified."

She growled but kept quiet. Despite his methods, he'd gotten her through.

Stars glittered in the night sky, reminding her of camping with her dad, and how he'd get her to name the star systems. It all looked so different in Bangladesh. The angles and positions weren't the same. She quickly found a few: Leo, Cassiopeia, Gemini. When had it turned so peaceful? Would another wind burst come for them before they reached Shaplapalli? No signal from her phone—not surprised. She tossed it on the floor, the muscles in her leg tensing to smash it.

"How much longer, Miss Clara?" Samira said.

"A few minutes," Clara turned and pasted on her official STC-trained smile. "Not too long."

Blake glanced at Clara a few times through the rear-view mirror. She waited for him to say something between the rough bumps, fallen trees, and loud engine groans. When he didn't say a word, she relented. "What is it?"

"I didn't expect you to come. You're either a great person, or you're bat-shit crazy being out here when a monsoon is going to hit any moment," Blake said in Bengali, the first time he'd bothered to speak to her in another language.

Elijah laughed. "She very edicated."

Clara couldn't decide if he meant dedicated, educated, or medicated.

"Miss Clara is bat-shit crazy, bat-shit crazy, bat-shit crazy," Samira laughed.

"She's not crazy," Farzana argued with a very stern face she'd normally saved for defending her friends when other kids made fun of them. "She's happy. Mom says people who act weird and say funny things are just really happy."

"Oh, you're *very* happy then," Samira pursed her lips and tilted her head, her brow raised exaggeratedly.

Blake sealed his lips to hold back a laugh, but his dimples gave away his amusement.

"Thank you, Farzana," Clara said like Nurse Priya might say, then she eyed Blake. "Can't be both? The sky is clear. We're fine."

"Not clear," he said, pointing out the window.

As if they'd passed into a different world, the stars disappeared behind dark clouds. *That doesn't make any sense.* The earlier storm that caused the microburst should have been long gone by then. This had to be something new. She felt a lump in her chest. "We can get to the school and take shelter there," she said.

He looked at her hard, for just a moment, then back at the road. His eyes said everything. *If we make it to the school.* As if the storm heard their thoughts, the wind picked up and slammed the truck hard enough for Blake to swerve off the road, narrowly missing a tree. Leaves and branches hit the truck like little dive-bombing birds. He slammed on the brakes. If the branches got any bigger, they'd break through the glass and their situation would get exponentially worse.

"Oh no. Oh no. We're going to die," Samira said.

"No good. No good," Elijah chanted, his hands pressed against the console.

"You might be right. Mom says bravery without wisdom is just recklessness in disguise," Farzana cried. "I don't know what that means but she said it when Dad took me to look for tigers and we nearly crashed and I think we're in trouble and we shouldn't have come here."

"We'll get through this," Blake flashed a genuine smile. "A little wind isn't going to hurt us. We're too strong for that. We'll wait here a few minutes then back up and continue down the road when it's not so windy. Copy?"

Farzana jittered, "Copy."

"Copy, we're dead," Samira said.

"Copy," Clara nodded, appreciating his calmness.

"Besides, look at all the medical supplies we have. We can all get hurt at least thirty times each before we run out. More lives than a cat."

The girls laughed nervously. They'd helped Clara pack the boxes, so they'd know there were plenty of bandages, but that wouldn't help if the wind flipped the truck or tossed it around.

Blake leaned over the front seat and put a hand on her shoulder. "We're okay," he said. His penetrating gaze made her swallow hard. "Those supplies will get to Shaplapalli before the monsoon hits. You're going to complete your mission."

His callused hand felt firm and reassuring.

"Take a few deep breaths," he said, leading by example with a few deep breaths of his own. "Just like this, girls. We take a deep breath in, hold for a few seconds, big breath out, hold for a few seconds. It will help you think when situations get scary. Works for me every time. Box breathing."

Clara breathed a few boxes and felt strangely grounded despite the wind and branches blowing against the truck. She only shrieked a few times when larger debris hit the window. *How long before it cracks the glass?* Elijah joined in on the breathing.

Finally, after ten minutes, the wind died down, and Blake pulled back onto the road. Not a minute later, they came upon a fallen tree with a trunk as thick as an ox.

"Are you serious?" Samira balked. "We're trapped."

"It's okay," Clara said, although she didn't think it was okay at all. They had nothing to cut down a tree that thick and no chance they could move it. It would be days before someone came out to chop it.

"What do you think? It's a mile or so to Shaplapalli?" Blake said.

Clara blinked. "What?"

"No sure," Elijah said, peaking out the front window at the sky as if it would tell him.

"A mile and a half?" Blake spun to the girls. "Do you know where we are? How much further to home?"

The girls glanced around the trees, seemingly more for his sake than any chance of recognizing one tree from another after a windstorm. They both shook their heads.

"Okay." He pulled out his phone and tapped the screen, but it must not have worked because he began frustratedly rubbing his hands on his pants. He stepped out of the truck, popped open the back, flipped the tarp up, went into his bag, and took out a large dark-green box with a screen on the front and an antenna at the top. It looked military. Maybe a GPS? And now she understood why Raj had given him the truck. He was a soldier, most likely on a mission. The request had probably come from well above Raj's head, forcing him to cooperate. They were either very safe with him or in a lot of danger.

Blake marched away while he played with the device. He held it up to the sky like it might catch a satellite if only it was a few feet higher.

The stars were back out, the worst of the storm had passed, and the wind had eased. For now.

"We go back?" Elijah said through chattering teeth. "No way get pass dis tree, so we can no get supplies to dem."

"It's half a mile," Clara said, climbing out of the truck.

Blake searched beneath the tarp for something.

"We can walk it. Clouds are gone, so it's safe," Clara said.

"We go back?" Elijah repeated.

Blake shrugged. "Up to you. I have to keep going."

# Chapter 5

"We don't know if it's any safer back there," Clara said. "If the wind picks up again...and a tree could have fallen behind us. Half a mile, if we hurry, will only take ten minutes. We can drive one of the local vehicles back this far and load up the supplies."

Blake nodded. It didn't matter to him. He was going to Shaplapalli, anyway.

Clara figured if there were no more fallen trees between them and Shaplapalli, they could still get the supplies. The girls stood stalk-still beside each other, more like little trees than children in the dark. She worried she was putting them in further risk, but she couldn't leave them there alone, even if taking them into a possible windstorm was just as dangerous. Why had she brought them with her? *Because if I got there with the supplies and not the girls, their parents would be furious with me. They'd panic. But the girls would be safe.*

"Okay, let's go."

"Miss Clara? I'm scared," Samira said.

"Mom says when I'm scared, I should remember that I'm smart and brave," Farzana said, placing an arm around Samira. "And if I listen to my heart, I'll know what to do." Farzana looked up at Clara. "My heart is beating really fast, telling me to get back in the truck."

Clara couldn't help smiling. She approached the girls but Blake stepped in front of her, kneeled, and drew them close.

"I know you're scared, but you've got to be brave now. Bravery isn't about not being afraid or having a slow, steady heartbeat; it's about facing your fears head on. Everything will work out. We won't let anything bad happen to you, okay? We promise," Blake said.

The way he spoke to the girls, like an uncle or a father, made Clara forget he was on a mission that didn't include helping these people. His gentle tone and encouraging smile made her feel safer, too. He strapped on a large blue hiking pack—definitely not military, but he probably didn't want to be too obvious. He brushed up against her as he walked by.

"Thanks. That was nice," she said.

"I mean it. We've got each other's backs, right? And I kinda like having you around. Let's get going."

She swallowed. *Liked having her around?* Clara watched him march ahead, the girls following close behind. She double-checked that the windows and doors were locked, taking a few breaths to sort out her thoughts. Did she like him around, too? It didn't matter. He'd be gone by sunrise, and she'd never see him again. She called to Elijah to follow behind her, hoping he'd see her request as a compliment that she trusted him to protect their backs.

They found no further fallen trees on the road, giving Clara hope the supplies could reach Shaplapalli before the monsoon hit. The moisture filled her lungs with the clean, crisp scent of freshly washed leaves. She swore she smelled cinnamon, reminding her of waking up to her mother's homemade cinnamon buns. Her mom had always known what to do when Clara felt like shit, studied too hard, or had a rough night.

Flashing police lights lit the forest in the distance and told them they'd reached Shaplapalli. They came upon another blockade, intended to keep people from leaving, not arriving. Two officers stood outside their cruiser on the other side of two A-frame barricades. Blake put his hand out to stop Clara and the girls from moving forward and sauntered ahead, taking a wide angle so as not to startle the police. It helped...a little. The officers still startled, stunned to have someone approach them from behind. Both officers instinctively reached for their pistols but kept them holstered when they realized Blake wasn't a threat and saw Clara and the girls standing on the road with Elijah.

The officer spoke Bengali. "Where did you come from? Are you okay, madam?"

Clara was used to being called madam but it still made her feel old, especially the way they said it. "We're fine. Tree fell on the road, so we had to walk."

"Very dangerous out here in the storm."

"I'm with STC. I have supplies for the school, but they're back at the truck. Can you help us get them?"

"No."

*Thanks for the consideration.*

The officer realized they weren't about to walk away. "We can't leave our position. Strict orders not to let anyone on the road."

Clara wondered if Blake had another wad of cash to give, but these two didn't look like they'd accept it. They were much younger than the other officers, their posture more erect. Their overcoats had no blemishes.

"If we find a car, will you let us get the supplies?" Clara asked.

"Strict orders not to let anyone on the road," the officer droned exactly as he'd said it the first time.

"I understand that. And I totally agree, for most people. But we're with the STC. That's Save the Children Foundation," Clara said like she took it personally they weren't acknowledging the importance of the STC. "Our mission is to deliver supplies to help the people in remote towns like this. What will happen to you if you get hurt in the next storm and there are no supplies? What do you think the doctors stationed at the school will do? They probably don't have enough for everyone if it gets bad."

The officers eyeballed each other.

Blake's eyes had been on the officer to the left as she spoke, whom she realized belatedly must be the senior.

"Okay. Okay," the officer on the left said in English. "If you find a vehicle and storm not here, we let pass."

Clara smiled and hugged the girls. They were safely near the school. If they could get the supplies into another vehicle, could she continue on to Shalbanpur tonight and distribute supplies to them? If the police let them go back and forth twice, she might make it back to Purnima. But she'd be going on her own. Blake had a mission, if he could get past the police barricade. If he couldn't get away, would he stay to help them? It caught her by surprise that she wanted him to. He'd saved her life. That's all it was. She'd forget him in a few days.

They headed for the school. She expected a small building for such a little village, probably a few hundred people packed like sardines inside, and her first glance proved her right. The second floor looked more like an attic than a complete second floor, but the bricklayer siding and galvanized iron sheets made it seem sturdier than the houses they'd passed. By her records, the school had been built three years ago, designed under budget for the monsoon season and thankfully built on an upward slope, drawing the water away from the building and down the gravel street.

Clara searched for vehicles with an insignia on the side, prepared to beg anyone with a company logo for help. Although they passed two vans, none had a logo. Most of the village used bicycles and scooters. *Small town.* It was nothing like Ventura or anywhere back home, really. Everyone in California seemed to own their own car, even if it was coated in rust. Even Purnima, not nearly as impoverished, had far more vehicles than Shaplapalli.

The moment they stepped inside the school, the girls ran off. On instinct, Clara shouted for them to come back but realized they were at home now and she was the stranger. She gave a small smile at the people gathered tightly in classrooms as she passed. Their stares lingered on her, probably because of her hair, a notable contrast to the black and dark brown hair of nearly everyone they passed. *White skin, short blond hair...about as far from relatable as I can get.* Even Blake blended better than she did. Maybe it meant she'd command more authority than the average person. Or they might see her as an intruder. She smiled her STC smile, nodding and saying hello to all the eyes that locked on hers. She turned to find Elijah had disappeared, maybe waiting at the entrance for them to return. Blake blew through the crowd so quickly she lost sight of him. She felt alone in the school until Samira and Farzana flew back into view with three other girls and two older women in tow.

"Thank you for bringing our girls home," the women said, probably Samira and Farzana's mothers. "We were worried sick."

"These two are wonderful children. It was my pleasure."

Both moms raised their eyebrows and laughed to each other, as if there might have been a mix-up and Clara was referring to the wrong two girls. Whatever hidden message passed between them went over Clara's head. Samira and Farzana gave each other conspiratorial smiles.

The pattering of rain hit the roof like a thousand tiny fingers tapping out a frenzied rhythm. The sound filled the room and blocked out all the noise from people talking. *No. No. No. Not yet. Not yet.* Sheltering in place wasn't supposed to be an option for her. She should be able to get supplies at least to another village. Maybe two. All she needed was a vehicle and the police to let them through...her through. Blake wasn't with her, even if she wanted him to be. *Light rain. I can get through a light rain.*

Clara peaked over the women's heads to see Blake talking to two large men, his hands waving in front of him as if he was doing sign language while he spoke. The two large men shook their head. *No.* Whatever he was trying to talk them into, they weren't interested. Clara thought she heard someone speak Urdu behind her, but when she turned to listen more carefully, she heard nothing and decided she'd been mistaken.

As if Blake felt her eyes on him, he sauntered over to her and said, "Those are the city bus drivers. They say they're done for the night. Storm is going to hit soon. Won't let us take the bus out there either. City property. They think we're crazy to go back."

She didn't care what they thought. Getting people the supplies they needed was all that mattered to her.

He read her defiance and sighed. "And there's nothing going out or coming in tonight. All vehicles are accounted for."

Clara shook her head. "Not good enough. I'm not letting those supplies float away in that truck." She meant it. With a sudden jolt of energy, probably from the momentum she'd already gained making bad decisions, she stormed over to the two men Blake had been speaking with. Her STC smile vanished, replaced with stern resolve.

"We need the keys to your vehicles to get supplies to these families. I don't care if you don't come with us," she said in Bengali, shifting her gaze from one man to the other. *There it was again. We.* Her determination seemed to make them more uncomfortable than Blake's muscles. "Give me the keys," she waved her fingers at them.

"Not our property," one man argued, the keys clutched in his hand.

"Tell your boss I stole the keys if anything happens to the van," she said. "Pickpocketed you."

"People need the vehicle for transportation. You damage it, and people will have no transportation," the other man said.

"If I don't get those supplies to people, some might die. I think people prefer being alive and cared for to having a drive down the road." Clara sounded harsher than she meant to, but she was tired of being questioned. She'd hoped her STC shirt would act as acknowledgement that she only wanted to help.

One man shook his head as he handed her the keys. "It's outside beside school. Be careful. Don't damage my bus. Oh, and the side door doesn't work. I'm getting it fixed tomorrow. It's jammed up."

She took the keys, gave a quick thank you, spun around and bumped right into Blake. He wrapped his hands around the back of her shoulders to steady her, his hard body and lips so close to hers she missed a breath. His eyes burned into her. Then he released her and stepped back. "Nice work," he said.

"We should get going before something else happens," she said. *Something else...*it sounded embarrassingly suggestive to her own ears. She couldn't help imagining him pressed up against her again.

They found Elijah leaned against the wall near the entrance, watching people, nodding and smiling when anyone looked his way. He seemed relieved when they strolled up to him and waved for him to follow.

They stepped out of the school's crowded warmth and into the frigid air. Part of her wanted to step back inside, find somewhere to sit, and wait out the storm. Nobody would blame her. But she'd blame herself for putting her own comfort over other people. Raj would want to know that she'd left him to help people from the community, not to sit on her hands and feel sorry for herself. Not to mention how embarrassing it would be for Blake and Elijah to do her job for her. She was the team lead. Elijah was one of her staff. Blake was...Blake.

The bus, more of a cargo van with extra seating, was a hundred feet away when Elijah fell sideways, collapsing onto the ground with a sharp howl of pain that might interest the local crocodiles if they were looking for easy prey.

"What happened?" Blake asked as he tried to help Elijah back to his feet, but the moment Elijah put weight on his left foot, he screamed.

"*Gorali*. Ankle," Elijah said.

"He rolled his ankle," Clara said. *We don't have time for this. He isn't any good to us now.* She felt terrible thinking so coldly, but what choice did she have? They needed to get those supplies and get back before the monsoon started or another microburst hit. It wasn't about her. *Goddamnit.*

Clara didn't have to say a word. Blake helped Elijah back to the school and returned running while Clara pulled the van around and pointed it toward the barricade where the police hopefully hadn't changed their mind.

"He'll be fine. Seemed better when we were inside," Blake said, coughing up phlegm. He opened the window to spit it out. Clara cringed as a line of spit trailed behind and fell onto his shirt. *Sexy.* He quickly brushed it off, not looking in her direction until they reached the police.

*He'll be fine.* Clara recalled the way Elijah's eyes had lingered on the girls a little longer than they should have; how he made for the back seat of the truck and reluctantly went to the front seat because

Clara had put pressure on him to do so; how he'd leaned against the wall when she saw him in the school, his eyes wandering. She assured herself he couldn't do anything in the school with so many people around. A girl wouldn't follow him anywhere.

"I thought you had to be on your way," she said, with no desire for him to leave but stupidly feeling like he might jump at the chance if she gave it to him.

"We're stuck in a storm," he shrugged, rolling the window up in big wide arcs. "They'll understand if I'm running a little behind."

His answer was as vague as his personality. He probably thought women loved the mystery. She didn't. Men with secrets were usually scumbags. "Where should you be headed? Once the monsoon hits, you'll be stuck here."

"I work for a development company," he answered, pulling back the lever of the front seat and reclining slightly. "Just a meeting to talk about land ownership changing hands. Prospective buyers want a price and sellers don't really want to leave."

"That's too bad," Clara said, keeping her eyes on the road as she drove toward the barricade. "Why would you want them to leave if they don't want to? Isn't it *their* choice?" *I know you're lying. You saved my life.* He was pretending to be a greedy bastard, but a greedy bastard would have gotten well out of the way to save himself.

"It's my job to convince them to move on to something better. Something different."

"So the STC lets you take their vehicles to conduct shady business?"

"Not a fan of business? Nothing shady about it. Raj and I go way back. Helped him out of a jam. Is that okay with you?"

"It's fine," she said, putting on her STC official smile. *Keep telling your lies, as long as you help me get the supplies to those people.*

They pulled up to the barricade, and the police waved them through. They continued down the bumpy road in silence, unimpeded until they reached the fallen tree. Stars and moonlight lit the van so well they barely needed headlamps to see and move between vehicles. Clara waited on one side of the tree while Blake retrieved the supplies on the other and handed them to her. Every time their fingers touched, she felt a spark and forced herself to forget it. He wasn't the right type of guy for her. She wanted someone that would put people above their own needs, care about the world—not the soldier type. Someone like...Raj. But he was married. Was Blake even available? He had no ring on his finger. A guy like him probably took it off before heading to a foreign country for business so he could mess around with local women.

Clara tugged sharply at the next batch of supplies Blake handed her. He turned and continued, as if he hadn't noticed. When they finished loading, Clara drove away the moment he sat in the passenger seat.

"And you're sure you're okay?" he asked, brushing the sweat off his face with the bottom of his shirt, which naturally gave her a good view of his abs and a scar along his side. It didn't look like a scar a man got selling real estate. *He's a soldier. Or maybe CIA? Who else has agents in the field in a place like this, just before a storm?* She couldn't ask him. Who knew what he might do?

"Fine," she said. Nothing about the way she felt was fine.

"You look tense. Long day for everyone. I hope Raj is okay."

"Yeah. Me too," she frowned. *And I actually care about him.*

A gust of wind hit the van from the right side, forcing her to pull hard on the steering wheel to stay on the road. The wind died so suddenly the van continued right, crashing into a small patch of thin trees before she could think to readjust. She swerved left back onto the road just in time to hit a deep rut. She swore it hadn't been there when they'd come through. Clara screamed as she fought to gain control, but the van popped up like someone was lifting the front end right before they crashed into a tree, air bags slamming into their faces, glass from the windshield shattering onto their laps. Medical supplies flew into the back of their heads like the storm scolding them to smarten up.

# Chapter 6

S team hissed from the engine. "Clara?" Blake groaned, as if he'd just woken up. Had she passed out?

"Clara?" More urgent this time.

"Yeah." Her shoulders and face hurt like hell, but they were alive—for now.

"Anything broken?" he said.

"I feel like I got smashed into a tree," she replied, chuckling at her own humor.

"Can you move?" Blake rustled beside her, but her eyes were barely open so she couldn't see what he was doing. When had she closed her eyes? When they hit the tree? How long ago was that?

"I think so."

Rain fell on the van like a jackhammer, rattling her bones with each impact. She touched her pounding head. A sticky substance had glued itself to her skull. When she brought her hand down, she saw blood caked to her palm, little tendrils of hair stuck to it. Her instinct was to scream. Instead, she took deep breaths, swallowing down the huffing that threatened to send her into a full panic attack.

Freezing water trickled down the broken branch that had smashed through the windshield and window, running down to her leg. A stinging sensation in her knee caused her to gasp. She touched the origin of the pain and felt a small piece of glass wedged into her thigh. Lifting her arm to do so also revealed a hundred small shards protruding from her shoulder, as if someone had taken a glass baseball and hit a home run directly into her shoulder.

"We need to stay dry," he said as he jerked the doorhandle and shouldered the door. It creaked open like an old rusted out truck. "We can get in the back seat for now. Take a minute to think."

"Blake," Clara said, reaching for his arm and grappling his shirt. "My arm. My leg. It feels pretty bad."

He moved the remnants of the airbag onto the dashboard, the glass crackling as he forced it down to hold it in place. A fresh wave of water poured onto her leg. This time she didn't feel the stinging pain.

"Shit. I'll come around and help you out." He leaned away, then twisted and said, "You've got this."

Blake jerked at the door, but the branch held it shut. His hand shook. If he didn't get out of the rain, he'd freeze. A thin emergency blanket would only do so much. *We're so fucked.* The supplies were getting compromised, she was in a world of pain, and they were far from any help. Nobody would come to rescue them. The police wouldn't allow it. Would the police come looking for them if they didn't show up back at the school in the next hour?

The rain picked up, driving into them like they'd parked beneath a waterfall. It was so dark. The only light she could see was the bobbing of Blake's headlamp as he worked at the door.

"Just pull me through to the back," she said, looking behind her at the splayed boxes of first aid kits and supplies. They'd have to crush them to take shelter back there. So many hours of careful counting and packaging.

Blake disappeared in the dark. She heard a tug on the side doors, then nothing. She nearly jumped when he yanked the back door open and crumpled the supplies, then slammed the door shut. "It's cold out there. How are you doing?"

Clara shivered. Water filled her lap and soaked her legs, so cold she couldn't feel the pain anymore. "Pull me. Let's get this done."

He threaded his hands beneath her armpits and pulled. She shrieked.

"Just keep going."

Glass crunched beneath her feet as she walked them backward, trying to get leverage to help Blake pull her through. It felt like he was ripping her arms off.

After, they lay pressed against each other, breathing heavy and shivering.

"Thanks," she said.

"Yeah. No problem."

"Where's your bag? Do you have a change of clothes?"

"Hid it away in the school. Didn't want to haul it around." He pulled off his shirt and draped it over the gap between the front seats like a curtain. It didn't cover the gap completely, but it would trap some heat—it wasn't good for much on their bodies, soaked through.

Clara pulled off her shirt and did the same, thankful she'd chosen to wear a sports bra that looked like a bathing suit top. "The guy who owns this van will be pissed. I hope he has insurance." Her teeth jackhammered as she spoke. "If we get out of this alive."

"We'll be okay. Do you mind? You're freezing and we need to stay warm." He pressed his chest against her back and wrapped his arm around her, careful to slink beneath her injured shoulder.

In any other situation, she might have laughed and shoved him away. *It's not so bad. We might stay warm enough to live through this.*

"Next move?" Blake said. "You're the expert."

She had a feeling he was giving her something to do, rather than being out of ideas himself. "We use a bunch of the emergency blankets and tape to block the windows and keep most of the wind out."

"Anything to eat?"

"There's nothing to eat in the supplies. The government already allocated extra food, oil and stoves to each village. I wasn't coordinating that group, but I saw plenty of food in the school when we were there." Clara clicked on her headlamp and sat up, doing her best to ignore the pain in her shoulder and leg. "The glass doesn't look too deep. We can pull the worst of it out with tweezers."

"Good plan. I'll start with the emergency blankets so we keep some heat in here. You find the tweezers, alcohol and gauze that you need. Once we have a decent shelter, we'll try to remove the shards. I don't think they're too deep, either." Blake pulled out an emergency blanket pack and wrapped it around her. He clicked his headlamp a few times, lowering the lumination. "Lets use as little light as possible. Don't know how long we'll be here."

Blake moved with ease and certainty, as if they were gathering cake ingredients. *We could die out here and he's so calm. He's got to be a soldier.*

"I don't suppose you have reception on your phone to make a call?" she asked. Maybe he had access to better tech. She thought of that green thing he'd used to figure out how far Shaplapalli was.

"Nothing," he said after peeking at his phone. "Left the good stuff in my pack."

"Do you have a radio? Another way to reach someone?" Clara lit Blake with her own headlamp.

Blake lifted his hand to block the light. "No. Why would I have a radio?"

"Forget it. You don't." She ruffled through the supplies strewn across the van. Gauze was easy to find; tweezers weren't. Two of the alcohol bottles had cracked and leaked onto the gauze and the van's vinyl seats. She couldn't tell if water or alcohol soaked the gauze, so she bundled them and put them aside.

"Ready?" Blake pulled a shard out of her shoulder before she replied.

She grunted and clenched her teeth hard instead of crying out, even though she really wanted to scream. The cold in her bones evaporated as the pain consumed her body and sweat dripped down her chest. Thinking she might chip a tooth before this was over, she bundled four popsicle sticks together and bit into them.

"Almost done with your shoulder."

There were a lot more shards in her shoulder than she thought; a dozen gauze pads with her blood on them lay in a second bundle. When Blake finished, he poured alcohol directly onto the cuts without warning. She snapped the popsicle sticks.

"Gonna need more popsicle sticks." She lifted the broken sticks to show him.

"You're doing really well. Tough as I thought."

"What, you think I'm tough?" She smirked.

He shined his light at her, forcing her to squint. "And a little reckless. Probably why we're here together."

She finally cried out when he unexpectedly pulled a larger piece of glass from her leg. That was the one she wasn't looking forward to. Some blood poured from the cut.

"Yeah, we're a couple of peas in a pod," Clara groaned. "Any glass I can pull out of your body? To test your toughness." No doubt in her mind he could take it.

"One thing I have more of than you," he said.

"What's that?"

"Luck." He yanked another piece out. It didn't hurt so bad. "Done." He poured alcohol on the cuts, forcing her to break another batch of popsicle sticks with her teeth, then he bundled gauze and wrapped her leg with a bandage.

"Thanks," she breathed. The chills came back the moment she relaxed and her temperature dropped. The emergency blanket wasn't doing enough. Blake had secured most of the space as they had planned, but when the rain and wind picked up, their makeshift wall fell down. Water submerged the front seats and soon the rest of the van would fill like a sectional bathtub. *Is this my luck or his luck now?*

"We need to find somewhere else to shelter."

Clara nodded. She had wondered who would say it first. They both knew the broken windshield and slight downward slope were going to screw them when the monsoon hit.

"I think I can walk." She winced when she lifted her leg. It was just pain. She could take it. She had to.

"We don't both need to wander around out there in this storm. I'll go. If I find a good place to shelter, I'll come and get you."

Clara immediately shook her head. "We can't separate." Her chest tightened with the thought of being alone, of Blake wandering in the bush, maybe dying, hit by a tree or blown into a rock face. She tried to steady her trembling hands, convincing herself it was the cold, not her fear. If leadership was a strength of hers, why did she feel so vulnerable? Why did he feel so safe?

He took her hand in his and squeezed. Some of the trembling subsided.

"I'm just cold," she said.

"I'll come back for you, okay? Nothing is going to happen to me out there. And nothing is going to happen to you in here." Blake sounded so sure of himself she might have believed him if she hadn't seen Raj crushed by a tent; Raj had seemed indestructible, too. *The storm doesn't care who you are or who you're trying to help.*

Blake smiled, squeezed her hand tighter, and then released it. It dropped to the floor, her knuckles striking the seat's plastic frame. He turned and disappeared into the dark, his shadow dissolving in the rain. Clara turned up the brightness on her headlamp, pressing her face against the backseat window, scanning for him. *He's gone. I'll be okay. I know I will be...* A gust of wind slammed against the van, knocking her off balance. She jerked to one side, bracing herself with her left arm, gritting her teeth against the searing pain.

The rain picked up, booming against the roof. Blake could be screaming for help ten feet away and she'd never hear him. Would they become a sad story, like the Collins family back in California? The police recovered the mom and kids frozen to death in their family car. Dad had gone for help. They found his body thirteen miles from the car, frozen and frostbitten. What about the Jacobs family? They died in the woods under a rock together, three miles from the highway. If not for the storm, they would have heard vehicles passing by. *Blake. You better get back here safely or I'm coming after you.*

Water pooled at the rear of the van, now coming in too fast to filter out. It wouldn't be long before it filled like a bottle. None of the training she'd conducted prepared her for this specific scenario. Shelter in place? Nope. Find cover? Not likely in these woods. There weren't any rock faces within miles. Walking to the school would be closer. Her teeth rattled. No amount of rubbing her hands together would bring the feeling back to her fingers. *This is how I'm going to die.*

Two more minutes. She'd give herself two more minutes before heading into the storm to find him. Two more minutes for Blake to get his ass back to her so they could get to a proper shelter. A minute later, fresh gusts of wind rattled the van. *Two more minutes, starting now.*

She counted the seconds. The wind came and went several times, never as strong as she'd felt at the hospital. Maybe the worst of the wind was done. *They just had to get shelter from this rain.*

Water snapped against her leg like a swarm of icy piranhas, each wave biting into her skin. She tried to pull away but the water found her wherever she tried to escape.

She nearly fell off the seat when something cracked against the window. A light shone into her eyes. *Rescue?*

Blake climbed in through the front door, an emergency blanket wrapped around him, doing seemingly very little for his vibrating body. "Fucking cold out there. It should be snowing."

*Snow wouldn't drown us. We'd build a nice little fire back here.* Clara imagined a flame in front of her, warming the inside of the van on a cold winter night. Snow would be so much better.

"Come on. I found a better place than this."

*We're going to be okay.*

With Blake's help, Clara climbed out of the van and into the heavy rain. Four spare emergency blankets filled her hands, and as she passed the glove box on her way through the passenger door, she popped it open and found a lighter. She hoped she could hold on to them; she couldn't feel them through her frozen fingers. One blanket dropped into the water and rode the current to the back of the van. Clara cursed, took as tight a grip on the lighter as she could manage, and let Blake heave her into the pouring rain.

*S-s-so d-damn c-cold.* "How far?" Clara heard her words slur in her mind. They walked down the road and turned into the trees. Every step hurt her leg. She didn't feel like she was in her body anymore. Instead, it felt like she watched herself from a distance. If she were viewing herself in a movie, she might think, *That girl has about five minutes to live.*

"Not far." Blake shouted through the rain. "We're okay."

*Good. Shelter isn't far. Then I can sleep. Blissful sleep.* She wanted to close her eyes so badly, she couldn't wait to hit the ground and snooze. A few more steps. "We can stop here," she slurred. They didn't need a shelter, she'd trained her mind to sleep anywhere. *Right here is good.* Her knees buckled and the earth lifted for her. Blake shoved it back down, taking her into his arms and carrying her.

"No sleep," he shouted, but all she could hear was the patter of rain against the emergency blanket and an urgent mumble in the distance, too far away to matter.

Blake wouldn't let her sleep. She swatted at him every time he shook her awake. *Why won't he let me sleep? What's wrong with this guy?* The scenery changed every blink: He carried her; placed her beneath a large overhang of trees; a little fire burned a few feet away; his body hugged hers. *Who the hell does he think he is?* There was no strength to fight him.

"Stay with me," he said whenever she tried to sleep. She clawed back at him to leave her alone, mumbling words of protest even she didn't understand. It didn't matter, he just had to let her sleep. Then she'd be fine.

Water dripped on the ground close to her head, pattering like her sink at home when she didn't tighten the faucet enough. *Landlord has to fix that. Remember to call him in the morning.* She asked Blake to go shut off the tap, but he ignored her. *Not the kind of guy to take orders from a woman, huh?* She swatted at him again.

"Let's hope the wind doesn't pick up, or we're finished." Blake rubbed her shoulder. What did it matter if the wind blew? Some branches would fall in the backyard?

"I'll pick it up in the morning," she said. "Stop making a big deal out of it."

She shivered again, cold despite being wrapped up in a blanket. Not her duvet, though. Something crinkly and not very warm.

A breeze blew the smell of wet soil and damp leaves into her face. "Close the window," she groaned. "It's cold in here."

"Not yet."

She felt him pull her tighter in his arms, caressing her, swaddling her. Finally, she drifted to sleep, and he didn't nudge her awake.

# Chapter 7

The wind blew the blanket out of her arms, snapping her awake. She couldn't see anything and fought to break free of the hands binding her.

"It's okay," Blake said. "It's me."

As if that would bring her comfort. Her throat constricted around the thousand tiny wings beating inside her chest. Her nose crinkled at the smell of must and body odor before she realized the smell came from her.

"What the hell is going on?"

"You were hallucinating. Hypothermia."

She wasn't home in her bed with Blake. Momentarily, she felt relief, until the memories flooded back into her mind and she realized the truth of their situation. "The wind is picking up." Blake didn't respond. Why would he? To say 'Thanks, Captain Obvious'?

He turned his headlamp on and hung it from a branch above their head. Water dripped into her eye when she looked up. She tried to wipe it away but couldn't capture the moisture with her bare skin. *Right. I took off my shirt because it was soaked.* "Do you know what time it is?"

"No. I dozed off too, and I don't like wearing watches. Thought this was going to be a quick in and out."

She started shivering again and pulled the reflective sheet tighter to her body. "What are we going to do?"

"Wait," he said. "Ride it out in here, unless we have to move. We're slightly elevated, so water will drain away."

"Elevated enough for the wind to catch beneath this shelter and blow it away." Clara realized how crass she sounded. "Thanks for saving my life again." She missed him pressed close to her and wished she hadn't shoved him away. It would be too awkward to get close to him now. *What would I say? 'Want to snuggle?'* She did.

He arranged tiny sticks into five separate bundles. She'd had the same training for heavy rain fires—gather bundles, burn through a batch of sticks, and replace them when needed. He pulled the lighter from his pocket and flicked it. "Fire died when I passed out," he said.

Clara wanted to cup her hands around the lighter and use the heat of the flame to warm them, but he held it under a few small sticks and waited until they caught. Before long, a small flame burned.

"It's still cold in here," he said after a long silence.

Clara swallowed down a smirk. "Well, we should probably get close again. Share body heat."

"Right." He didn't hide his crafty smile.

She knew nothing about him. Given the situation, she didn't have to. "So, where were you supposed to be heading tonight?"

"India. Crossing over for business."

"Right. Real estate." She hoped he'd pick up on her eye roll through her tone.

"Don't believe me?" he said matter-of-factly.

"I know a soldier when I see one," she said without a clue whether he was a soldier, a spy, or a special agent. What she knew was that he wasn't a real estate guy. He didn't dress or act like one. No way would he be going through small villages to get to India when he could take a direct flight to whatever major city he was selling in.

"Ever hear the saying, 'If I told you I'd have to kill you'?"

"Yeah, in the movies. Nobody says that," she ribbed.

"Nobody that lived," he stressed.

Clara laughed and felt a vibration from his chest as he laughed too at his own joke.

"Where are you from?" she said. "Or is that classified intel?"

"Highly classified. I'm from California."

She huffed. "Sunny beaches and surfing?"

"Beautiful women and gorgeous mountai—"

She felt Blake twist away from her. A light bounced slowly in the distance, maybe from where they'd parked the van. The veil of rain made it hard to tell how far away it might be. Another light near the first popped up, bouncing wildly, maybe a headlamp on someone that couldn't see the trees in front of them. Clara took in a breath, prepared to shout for help. Blake covered her mouth with his large, dirty hand, and she crushed sand between her teeth like rock candy without the satisfying sizzle.

"No," he whispered. "We don't know who it is."

He turned off his headlamp and knocked the fire out into the rain. Clara held still as he pulled his hand away, retreating into the dark.

"That's crazy. Nobody out here is going to hurt us." She took in another deep breath, and again, he placed his hand over her mouth, firmer this time. What felt so safe and comfortable twisted in her gut.

"Trust me," he said.

"Mm...Mmm," she mumbled *no* and tried to pull his hand away. He leaned over her, pressing down on her with his weight to keep his hand in place.

"Trust me," he enunciated, giving no space for discussion. She would have liked to point out this wasn't the best method for building trust, then figured he wouldn't care either way. His eyes narrowed on the lights like a cat's watching a mouse scurry around, prepared to pounce.

"They might kill you," he said before she could muster a scream. He slowly pulled back his hand from her lips.

Clara forced the words through clenched teeth. "Because people hunt real estate agents during a monsoon?"

He frowned. "Fine. I'm not a real estate agent. Stay here."

"What? You're seriously leaving me?"

He stalked into the rain, raindrops pouring down his bare back. A third light joined the other two. No way was anyone hunting them out here. Someone had come to help. Blake had to be mistaken.

She pulled the emergency blanket tight around her and stood. When she thought she saw him fall, she limped after him. The cold water took her breath away. *This is a mistake.* But she had to check on him. If he was a soldier, maybe he was having flashbacks or something, thinking there were rebels hunting him. He could hurt them before he realized they were trying to rescue them.

She crouched low, wanting to get a closer look before revealing herself, then realized the emergency blanket would stand out like a beacon if they flashed their lights toward her. She ditched it. The pain in her leg wouldn't let her crouch for long so she stood, choosing to stand tall like another tree rather than a small rock on the ground. The three sets of lights that had gathered in one place now moved in three separate directions. They'd found the van and were searching for survivors. *They're here to help us.* If she believed that, why didn't she shout for help? Because the pouring rain would mask her voice.

*Because Blake saved my life twice and he thinks they might be dangerous. What if he knows something I don't?*

One light flashed directly on her and she froze, stiff as a tent pole bracing against a gale. The light started bouncing toward her. If whoever held it said anything, she didn't hear it until a man's voice shouted as he closed the gap between them. He wore a poncho with the hood pulled over his head and a headlamp worn overtop.

He pointed at her, and she couldn't tell if he had a gun in his hand. The rain seemed to stop as she waited for the flash of a muzzle and the sharp punch she imagined a bullet felt like.

An arm wrapped around the man's neck. *Blake.* The man's hands shot up, pulling at Blake's forearm to break loose. Blake pulled him backward off his feet, and the man went limp.

Her hands shook and her eyes burned. "Is he dead?"

Blake stepped over him, skin shining in the light of the fallen man's headlamp. "Sleeping. Come on, we have to keep moving."

"Who was he? Did you kill him?" She asked again as Blake dragged her away from the fallen body. She fought to break free, but his grip was too tight. The other lights were gone. Had he killed them too?

He snapped her around to face him and placed his lips inches from her ear, both hands gripping hers. "He's not dead. We will be if we don't keep moving."

"Then let me go." She wanted nothing to do with whatever he had going on. Helping people. That's what she did. People didn't get hurt because of her, they got help. "Let me go." She tugged harder when she saw the gun in his hand. She yelped from the pain in her arm, and he let her go.

"I'm sorry you saw that. They came here looking for me. I can't explain why." He sounded regretful. "That won't stop them from hurting you. Killing you is a stepping stone to me. They saw us to-gether in Shaplapalli."

"Who are you?" she hissed.

A faint flash a short distance away followed a sputter on a tree beside Blake's head. Clara dropped, crashing her knee hard against a stone, and screamed. All she wanted was to be home in bed. No Blake, no men with guns, no pouring rain…no pain.

Blake lifted her onto his shoulder as pieces of tree blew apart around them. She finally heard the shots. *Bang. Bang. Bang.* In quick bursts of three. Blake returned fire, carrying her further into the forest, away from the van and anyone that could help them. Running into the bush was a death sentence in the coming monsoon. They had no supplies and no clothing.

The skin on her oblique rubbed raw over the minutes he carried her before he finally put her down beneath a fallen tree's roots. The roots were so large it created a slight barrier from the rain. She'd bit her lip twice and tasted blood in her mouth, the rainwater unable to wash it out for her.

Clara lifted herself onto her side and grit her teeth. "What do we do? Fight them? Blake? Blake?"

Blake sat facing away from her, shivering, rubbing his hands to-gether. She crawled over and wrapped the emergency blanket around him. The sides were torn, though it was effective enough to provide some warmth.

"Blake." Clara did her best to sound resolute. Action is what she needed, a focus. Despite the protection from the rain, she saw a liquid pooling on the ground beside his leg. "Have you been shot?" She considered releasing him to check on the damage. If he wasn't so cold, and if she had any emergency supplies, she would have.

"Flesh wound," he muttered through chattering teeth.

"If you lose too much blood, it doesn't matter what you call it." She bumped backwards and tore away at her pant leg below the bandage where the glass had struck her. A few sharp tugs and the bottom half of her pants tore free. She ignored the pain in her shoulder—it wasn't important. Clara scooted around, twigs and branches jabbing her thighs and butt, and she wrapped the strand of cloth around his leg and pulled tight.

"That should slow the bleeding."

"Thanks. We should keep moving." Blake grunted and twisted away from her to his knees. "They won't stop until they find me."

"They must really want to buy that property." Her words hung in the air for a few moments before they both laughed.

"They're with ISI. Inter-Service Intelligence. Pakistan's version of the CIA or the UK's MI6. We disagree with the handling of a target."

"Like the CIA? Doesn't that make them the good guys?"

He shrugged. "There aren't any good guys, just different points of view."

"And what's your point of view? US military?" Soldiers tried to hide in plain sight, but they stood out, always too sure of themselves. As if his beard and messy hair would throw anyone off. Maybe fifty years ago. The way he spoke like his word was unquestionable...and how he moved, like he carefully measured every step...

"I stuck around too long. I put people at risk." It didn't answer her question, but his words came out hard, like he was angry at himself.

"Why did you?"

"What?" He seemed confused, like they hadn't just been talking to each other.

Clara glanced at his leg, confirming he wasn't losing too much blood. He might be in shock. "Why did you stick around when you could have left after I saw you in the tent? You might have missed the microburst."

Blake leaned back and stared at her, thinking. Her stomach did somersaults as he dug his eyes right into her. But then his head snapped to the forest, his body stiffened, and his ears perked up. She followed his line of sight, hearing nothing but raindrops striking leaves, seeing nothing but the gloomy forest trees.

"They're searching for us," he whispered.

Or were they looking for their friend he'd killed—put to sleep. "How many of them are there?"

Blake didn't have time to respond. Dark figures crashed through the bush, shouting at them. At least one of them was a woman. Clara recognized some words in Urdu, but not enough to know what they were saying. Blake didn't move, so she didn't either.

Before she realized what was happening, a man took her by the hair and pulled her away from Blake. She screamed from the sharp pain before the woman cracked Blake in the head with something in her hand, then spit at him. *That looked personal.*

The ISI forced them forward, one man keeping Clara's head wrenched back while another shoved Blake ahead. They cussed at them in Urdu. At least their anger felt less pointed since she had no idea what they were saying, but that didn't soften the sharp tugs at her hair which tore the strands out of her skull while she stumbled through the trees, crying and falling every few steps. Foreign agencies had always been good to her. Why were the ISI being so cruel?

In their ruined van, the man Blake had knocked out sat pressed against the wheel, holding his head. He seemed untroubled by the pouring rain, like it wasn't happening. The woman cracked Blake behind the knee and he grunted as he hit the ground. Clara couldn't tell how bad his wound was, but he had to be in a ton of pain. The bullet was probably still in there.

"What your mission?" the man holding his head asked her in English.

Without thinking, she said, trembling with each word, "Every child deserves a future. In the United States and around the world, we give children a healthy start in life." She realized they wanted to know about Blake's mission, not hers. They thought she was part of it. That might be why she wasn't dead yet.

"She is not a soldier," Blake said loud and slow. "She is a good person. Helping children. Supplies are in the van. Look."

The woman stuck her head through the driver's door and scanned inside with her flashlight. She spoke in Urdu to the others. Clara wondered if Blake knew what they were saying. His eyes peered like he was translating their conversation. To her, the pattering of leaves would disguise their words even if they spoke English.

A light flashed from down the road and everyone froze. *More people?* She thought they'd die alone. If they kept wasting time, they'd all die together. They didn't respect the storm, and that might kill them all. *The storm doesn't care about your mission.*

The light bobbed closer, like someone walking casually down the street in downtown Ventura. It came within a dozen yards and stopped.

"All okay?"

Relief and fear buzzed through Clara, and she let out a deep breath that might have included a little bit of a manic laugh. Elijah limped forward.

The others stared, seemingly too stunned to move. The woman broke the silence, shouting at Elijah. He paused and turned off his headlamp, then raised his hands into the air.

"You not come back for hours. I know something wrong. You not give up."

"They're trying to figure out who he is." Blake shuffled backward on his butt. All three had pistols pointed at Elijah. Two of them had fully faced away from Clara and Blake, but the third only half so. *Come on, look the other way.* If they could only get a moment without everyone watching, they could put some distance between them, maybe fight back. *Right. Grab a branch and home-run a bullet coming for my head.*

"No move," the man commanded Clara in English.

"Let us go." She tightened her fists.

"No shoot," Elijah said, then spoke two distinct words in Urdu.

The man facing away from Clara spoke to the girl beside him and waved her forward. She tightened her grip on her gun and moved toward Elijah. Clara wanted to warn him. Elijah had no idea what he'd stumbled into. Would the woman shoot Elijah for no reason? How could this be Pakistan intelligence if they were so willing to kill people?

A shadow creeped to Clara's left, deep in the woods. At first, Clara thought it was a large animal. If not for her leg, she might have run on pure instinct. The shadow slowed and paused, now appearing more like a tree in the distance. Clara watched closely, wondering if she'd imagined it. Then it moved again. *Who's out there?* She almost shouted it.

"No shoot," Elijah repeated in English, then again in Urdu. All the ISI had turned on their lights, illuminating Elijah who still had on his stupid straw hat and no shirt. He didn't seem cold yet, but he would be soon.

One of the ISI flashed their light into the bush to Clara's right. Then he twisted, pointing his gun at Blake's face and shouting. In two strides, his gun slammed the side of Blake's head. Clara heard a distinct metal click she'd only heard in a movie. *Oh God, they're really going to shoot him.*

She stood and shoved the man.

He tripped. The other two in front spun. Then at least six lights came on. Men shouted from all around her. Multiple flashlights lit up all three ISI members. Even the rain seemed to freeze among the tension.

"Get down," Blake told her. He'd come up close and pulled at her pants to bring her to the ground.

The ISI agents lowered their weapons. Clara didn't trust they'd give up that easily; this wasn't an action novel.

"Who are they?" Clara said.

"Friends."

The men surrounding them closed the distance to ISI, placed their hands behind their backs, and ziptied them.

"All okay?" Elijah asked again when he reached her.

She wrapped her arms around him. "Thank you."

Two men lifted Blake to his feet.

"You broke van," a deep voice bellowed from the van. "You break, you bought. That how they say it in America?"

She laughed, nodding as she released Elijah and limped over to hug the big man. "Thank you for coming."

"My van. Came for it," he said in a matter-of-fact tone. His body was as rigid as his personality, rifle slung over his shoulder.

Another of Clara's saviors stood pencil-thin, nearly disappearing at the angle of the trees. "YOU BROKE VAN!" a woman shrieked.

"My wife," the big man grumbled.

Clara released her grip and limped to give her a hug, too.

"She's been in the hugging mood all night," Blake said. Another rescuer tossed him a poncho, and he flung it at her. She threw it over her emergency blanket, trying to gather as much heat as she could.

The rain continued as they walked together. The big man let Clara lean on him so she could keep up with the others. Another of her rescuers helped Blake. "Where is your vehicle?"

"Up road. Tree collapsed."

*Damn, that means they won't get the supplies.* "How far?"

"Not far."

Clara regarded the van. "Can we take the supplies? Some of them? They're going to need them."

The big poncho hood shook. "Elijah said you put self in danger for other people. Very noble. But you put more in danger, too. All thing must be measure. We would not come if we not owe Elijah. You are lucky."

*Elijah.* She'd thought he might have stayed behind to ogle the girls. She'd judged him wrong. Maybe because he fit the television profile of a sleazebag? Or because Raj had briefed her to watch out for men that could take advantage of her or other young women? Since she'd met Elijah, he'd been a good worker. *Just...different.* She'd had no reason to doubt him.

Her eyes flew back to the supplies in the van. "A bag?" she begged. "I'll carry."

He laughed. "You cannot carry self."

"Please?" If she didn't make it back with at least a pack, all of this would have been for nothing.

"Ugh, I have pack in van."

She could have kissed him if he wasn't out of reach. "Thank you."

Four of her rescuers marched at the front, two leading the way, followed by the three ISI and two behind. When the rain slowed, Elijah fell back beside her. They limped together. "Thank you. For rescuing us."

"It my job."

They reached another van, nearly identical to the one they'd crashed. A heated discussion took place between the big man and his wife. His wife threw up her hands, stomped to the driver's seat, and slammed the door. The back seats were down, making it easy for the soldiers to bundle up together with the ISI in the middle. When Elijah poked his head in the van, the big man's wife yelled and threw a bag at him. Then another. The big man shook his head as he walked by. Clara had gotten him into trouble.

She sat on the van's hard floor. Blake pressed up against her again to make room for the others.

"You saved my life."

"Yeah. I did." She rested her head on his shoulder. "I think I still owe you one, though." She felt his eyes on her and smiled.

# Chapter 8

Dr. Kendra sat at the edge of the cliff, watching the waterfall cascade down. She seemed lost in thought. Had therapy ended?

"Dr. Kendra?"

"It's remarkable how extraordinary situations can lead to equally extraordinary human connections," Dr. Kendra said, wiggling her toes in the water's mist.

"Or how disconnected situations can lead to equally detached humans. That day wasn't all about the boys and their needs." Clara could hear the anger in her tone as she voiced her thoughts. "We used to go away together, and he'd forget about the job and really be with me."

Doctor Kendra turned toward her. "How much do you think you've changed since then? You certainly seem like a different woman."

Clara forced a smile. She had changed. She remembered wanting to help people; it was her job. Reliving the experience, though...she'd been so impulsive, just like Blake. And it felt so good. So freeing. "I might have changed a little. Of course. I have a family, for god's sake. Responsibilities."

"Do you resent him for not changing? Do you feel like you're alone in all the responsibility?"

Of course she did. She'd grown up, and he'd gotten to stay a soldier, caring for her less as the years went on. "Maybe."

"Did Blake tell you what he was doing in Shaplapalli that day? Why he hadn't left for India sooner?"

Clara swallowed hard. She had a feeling Doctor Kendra was about to tell her something that would destroy the memory for her. *Tell her you don't want to know. It's not worth it.* "No, he didn't."

"Elijah was an agent with the CIA, operating under the guise of assisting the STC. Even his façade, which I found equally unsettling, was calculated. He acted in ways that might seem odd or off-putting, playing into stereotypes of the eccentric or socially awkward foreigner. This kept eyes off his real agenda and made those who might question his presence dismiss him as harmless or irrelevant. During his mission, he overheard a conversation about the ISI planning to eliminate a US Special Forces unit. He did some digging and discovered the ISI planned to kill Blake's team when he reached them in India—they didn't agree with his mission. Geopolitical tensions."

Doctor Kendra brushed the mist off the top of her legs like she was giving Clara time to jump into the conversation. *Just tell me.* "Elijah reported what he'd heard up the chain and met with Blake to warn him as Blake traveled through Purnima to India. According to the report, Blake wanted to protect his team from the ambush, so he delayed his departure to work with the STC so the ISI could catch up to him. He planned to take them out. Nobody expected the storm to hit early."

Clara felt bile rise in her throat. "So, we only met because he was protecting his team. The boys, again. It wasn't about me. All this time..." Her fists clenched and tears sprang down her cheeks, completely unwanted.

"Yet, it was a very noble thing to do, don't you think? I can see why you feel him staying behind wasn't about you at all, but I wonder if there might be room for both motivations—protecting his team and being drawn to you."

Clara cringed but didn't respond.

"Think about it again. He met you, and when he should have left Purnima for Shaplapalli so the ISI would follow him deeper into the forest and away from people, he hesitated. Why do you think he hesitated?"

"Did Blake tell you?" Clara splashed some water on her face to disguise the tears.

"He made a poor judgment call because he wanted to spend a few extra minutes with you. Nobody would admit this, but his men fudged the timelines so the army wouldn't know. He might have been court-martialed. If the army knew he'd risked the mission to be with a woman..." She paused, letting that sink in. "For a man like Blake, trained to put the mission above everything, to never deviate from protocol—this wasn't just breaking rules. This was probably the first time in his career he'd ever let personal feelings override his training. That's not a small thing."

Clara forced a smile. Blake hadn't changed at all. But he'd loved her back then. She felt it. Now...?

Clara sat beside Doctor Kendra. "We were both so honest about our feelings for each other. For all the secrets he had to keep from me, I thought we would never lie to each other."

"Bonds that might take months or years to develop can be forged in moments. The nature of military operations requires secrecy and discretion for safety and strategic reasons. But he didn't lie to you. He only held back the military operational situation. And I'm not saying that was right of him, especially after all those years, but it's what the army expected of him."

Clara leaned back on her elbows. Doctor Kendra sounded just like Blake had, making excuses for not opening up. "God, I hate when Blake talks like that."

"I know this is hard for you. That's completely understandable given what you just learned. You expected him to change who he is. Did you think he might settle down with a family and leave his job with the teams?" Doctor Kendra's questions were honest ones, spoken with little emotion. She wanted the facts. *What* had *I expected?*

"You're the doctor. You tell me." Clara asked with soft-spoken honesty.

"Men in his line of work have a hard time slowing down. The constant pressure rewires them—makes them feel more alive, more vigilant, when the stakes are highest." Doctor Kendra placed a hand on top of Clara's. "Over time, normal life feels foreign. A quiet dinner at the table becomes more challenging than a firefight. The skills that keep them sharp in the field make it almost impossible to relax at home." She squeezed Clara's hand. "He loved you. I think he still loves you. You both have a lot of hard compromises to make if you expect your relationship to work. He will have to learn to let work go sometimes and be present, put you and Sophia first. And you may have to give him time and understanding to change."

Shortly after that monsoon with him, they'd met up in different countries whenever they could, sharing a room together in a balcony hotel. His lips, his touch, the tickle of his beard…it was so exhilarating.

"I'm ready to go back now," Clara said. They had a lot of work to do if they had a chance of finding that place in their relationship again. If she could hold on to the memory of what they were…

The waterfall disappeared and the Genesis went black.

# Author Note

*Monsoon Rendezvous* began as a short story, but as the characters and world grew, I realized it needed more space to fully capture Blake and Clara's journey. The inspiration came from *The Genesis Project* and a comment Clara made about meeting Blake in a foreign country during a monsoon.

Writing this novella turned out to be one of the smoothest experiences I've had, requiring fewer rewrites even after feedback from my developmental editor, beta readers, and copy editor. What you're reading now is very close to the original draft, with just a few adjustments—like Elijah becoming an operative and joining their journey. In the initial version, Elijah simply reappeared at the end, having been absent since creeping out the girls at the start.

Exploring the dynamics between these characters against the backdrop of a raging monsoon was both fun and rewarding. I hope you enjoy the tension, camaraderie, and heart that went into this story. Thank you for joining me in this world!

# Acknowledgements

This novella wouldn't have been possible without the support and hard work of many incredible people.

A special thanks to my developmental and copy editor, Ayden Rails, for your honest and thoughtful feedback, for helping refine the book blurb, and for your input as the cover came together. Your expertise has been invaluable.

To my beta readers—Ione Jayawardena, Ludmilla Dubuisson, and Nikki Kennedy—thank you for your keen insights and encouragement. My books are better because of you.

Finally, to my Kickstarter backers—your belief in *The Genesis Project* helped bring this novella to life. Your support means more to me than I can express.

# Book Review

If you enjoyed this book, please consider leaving a book review. It means the world to Mark and helps other people find his books. As an indie author, it's essential to getting noticed online. Without a massive marketing budget, an indie author's next best resource is reviews.

Thank you so much.

# Free Short Stories

Want two FREE short stories? Download Mark's military thriller short story Operation Sanitation & Operation Tangle FREE!

## Download Now

# About the Author

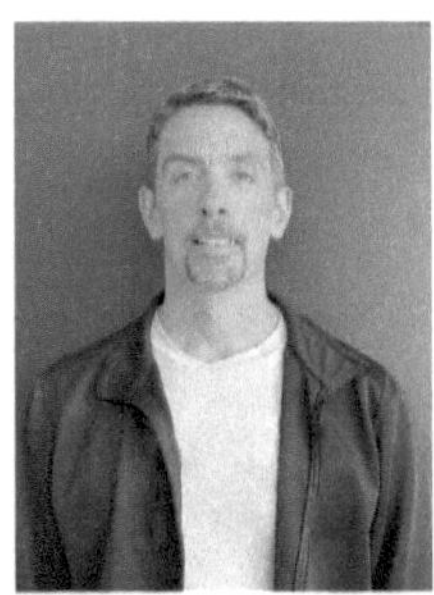

Mark PJ Nadon's life as a writer began when he read *The Scions of Shannara* and was so enamored with the story, the world and the characters that he wanted to write one of his own. It took Mark eight years to finish his first fantasy story and twenty-five more years to finish ten more novels. He lives in Ottawa, Canada and mainly writes thrillers in the military, post-apocalyptic, dystopian and fantasy genres.

When he isn't writing, Mark runs a fitness company, a dog sitting company, rock climbs and plays video games with his son Matthew.

# What's Next?

The adventure doesn't have to end yet! You can buy The Genesis Project, the full length novel that inspired this short story.

When a military PTSD treatment program starts leaving bodies in its wake, one soldier must choose between following orders and uncovering a deadly conspiracy—before his own family becomes the next target.

Buy The Genesis Project Now

Follow Mark on social media

## Check out Mark's website

www.ingramcontent.com/pod-product-compliance
Lightning Source LLC
Chambersburg PA
CBHW021749190726
48290CB00008B/2540